P9-DBL-946

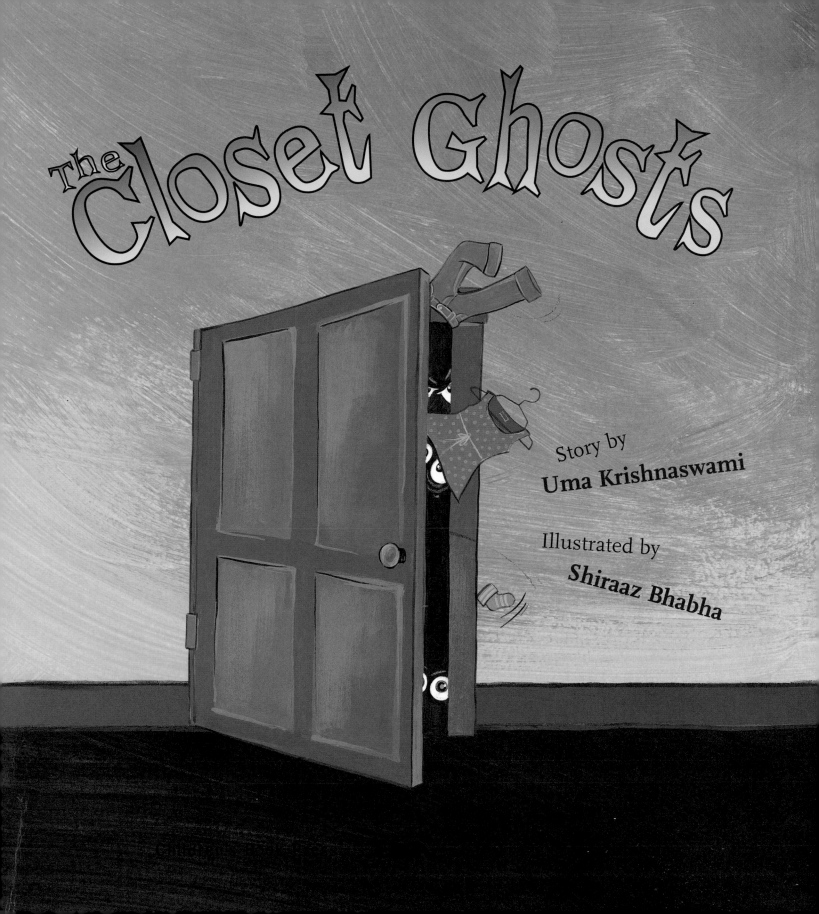

The Closet Ghosts

Story by
Uma Krishnaswami

Illustrated by
Shiraaz Bhabha

Mamma and Papa said she'd get used to it, but the new house felt all wrong to Anu. The echoes in the hallway made her shiver. She missed her old neighborhood. She missed her best friend Mira. She tried to call Mira but the phone wasn't working yet.

Worst of all, the closet in Anu's room had ghosts.

The ghosts pulled Anu's clothes off their hangers. They turned her socks inside out. They toppled her little statue of Hanuman the monkey god.

Mamma carried boxes into Anu's room. "Mamma," Anu said, "there are ghosts in my closet."

"Are you sure?" asked Mamma. "I don't see any." And off she went to unpack more boxes.

5

The next day, Anu went to her new school for the first time. She didn't know anyone, and no one knew her. She sat down at the wrong desk. "That's my desk," said a girl named Brianna.

"I'm sorry," said Anu. She waited for Brianna to say, *That's all right,* but Brianna went right on talking to the girl next to her.

In Anu's old classroom, she would have sat next to Mira. Mira would have talked to her.

Anu couldn't wait for the end of the day at this nasty new school.

That night the ghosts leaped and danced about in Anu's closet. They sang a ghostly song:

"Ha-ji-ha, we're ghosts
with backward-pointing feet.
With hairy-scary frowns
the human world we greet."

"Go away," said Anu. She tried not to listen to their scary howls and growls. "Hanumanji," she said to the statue on her shelf, "you have magical powers. Can't you drive these ghosts away?"

Finally, Anu fell asleep.

* In Hindi, a language of north India, when you want to speak respectfully to someone, you add the syllable "-ji" to the person's name. That is why Anu calls Hanuman the monkey god "Hanumanji."

In the morning, Anu heard a knock on her window. On the ledge outside was a large monkey. He swished his long tail. He cleared his throat and thunder echoed all around. "Ghosts and demons come not near!" he sang.

Anu opened the window. She was so excited she almost fell out.

"Hanumanji!" she cried. "I'm so glad you're here."

Anu offered lemonade and peanuts and fruit to Hanuman—respectfully, the way you're supposed to welcome a special guest.

She thought, *Please, Hanumanji, help me get rid of those scary ghosts.*

That afternoon, Anu went shopping with Mamma and Papa. They came back with things for the house, and a bag of marbles for Anu.

Anu said, "I think I'll build a rollercoaster for Hanumanji."

"Really?" said Papa.

"Yes, he's come to stay with us for a while," Anu told them.

"Imagine that," said Mamma, giving Papa a look.

"Unbelievable," said Papa.

That evening, Anu built the rollercoaster. "What a kind and clever girl you are," said Hanuman.

Anu told Hanuman about missing her old house, and school, and neighborhood, and her best friend Mira.

He said, "Not to worry. Your problems will disappear like ghosts in the night!" He spun the marbles down the rollercoaster, so fast it made Anu dizzy to watch.

She thought, *Shiver and shake, you mean old ghosts. I've got help.*

That night, Anu woke up needing to go to the bathroom. She lay in bed, listening.

Hanuman snored gently. Then the night fell silent. Not a ghostly peep broke the quiet. *Maybe he drove them away already,* Anu thought.

Anu crept out of her room, keeping close to the walls as she went down the hallway. She felt for the bathroom door. There it was! She turned the knob, went inside, and ran— *dhoom-dharaam* —into a tall shape with one long arm. Anu tried to scream, but her voice could only make a frightened squeak.

In a panic, she felt for the light switch.

Anu found the switch, turned it on—and stared! The hall closet smelled of new wood and soap.

Silly, Anu told herself, making her way to the bathroom at last. *You still don't know your way around this house.* From down the hall, she thought she heard the ghosts stirring. Bumps and thumps and "Ha-ji-ha!" floated down the hallway.

Anu couldn't be sure, but she thought she could hear Hanuman snoring underneath the racket.

The next day Anu dragged herself to school. When she got there she was surprised to find that everyone was waiting for her.

Brianna held out a tray of cookies. "It's my birthday," she said, "and you get the first cookie because you're the newest kid in our class."

"Wow," said Anu, surprised. "Thank you."

Later, at recess, Anu played tag with Brianna and her friends. They told each other jokes. They found words that rhymed and made them into songs.

Anu thought, *Maybe I could get used to this school.*

That afternoon, Anu said to Hanuman, "Do you think I could ever be friends with those ghosts?"

"Friends with ghosts?" said Hanuman. "What an original idea! Certainly worth trying."

Anu pictured the ghosts coming out of the closet and becoming her friends. So she picked some flowers for them. She found a blue jay feather and a speckled leaf. She made a bouquet.

But the ghosts ripped up Anu's bouquet and scattered the bits about. They shouted:

"Ha-ji-ha, we're no fools,
you can't make friends
with scary ghouls!"

That night, as Anu fell asleep, she knew she had to dream up a whole new plan.

$$2/7 + 4/7 = 6/7$$

$$\begin{array}{r} \overset{2}{1}9 \\ \times 3 \\ \hline 57 \end{array} \quad 2+12=14$$

Anu's new plan bubbled and simmered throughout the following day. She took it to school in her mind and thought about it in between doing other things. It got bigger and better during spelling and reading. It got polished as she took a math quiz.

At recess, when the kids played at rhyming words, Anu made up a whole new song for her new plan. She could hardly wait to put it to work.

After school, Anu brought out her drums.
She put on her dancing ankle bells. She threw
open the closet door.

Before the ghosts could sound out a
single scary word, Anu burst into her
very own song. She pounded her drum.
She stamped her feet. She sang:

"Ghostie-toasties come and hear
jokes to make you laugh and cheer.
Ha-ji-ha, come sing along,
join me in my funny song!"

A long moment of silence followed.
Then, "Hai, hai!" the ghosts shrieked.
"Funny-sunny people make us
quiver-shiver!"

Hanuman laughed and cheered.

The ghosts scurried out of the closet. With mumbles and groans, they hurried across the floor. Then they swooshed out of the window and up into the sky, and they were gone.

Anu looked around. "Well," said Hanuman. "That's that."

"Thank you," said Anu. "You helped me understand."

"Help, shelp," said Hanuman. "You did it all yourself. Well, I'd better get going now. I think I'm needed somewhere else." And he vanished in a flash of golden light, leaving behind the faintest trace of laughter.

All at once, the new house felt like a friendly kind of place.

The next morning, the phone rang.

"It's for you," Mamma said. "It's Mira."

"Anu, hi! I miss you," Mira said. Her voice sank to a whisper. "You'll never believe what's been happening. I have ghosts in my closet!"

Anu nearly dropped the phone. She grabbed at it in time to hear Mira say in amazement, "Oh my gosh. I've got to go. There's someone knocking on my window!"

Anu hung up the phone. Slowly, a little hum breaking out inside her, she began to get ready for school.

About this story

Although Anu and her family and friends are made-up characters, I didn't make Hanuman up. He is an important figure in the Hindu mythology of India. Stories about him have been told for thousands of years. When families like Anu's come to America, they bring these stories with them.

Hanuman is bold and brave. He can change his size, from tiny to giant, in the blink of an eye. He is a loyal friend and servant to the god prince Ram, or Rama, and his family. He is thought to protect people from wicked ghosts and goblins.

A 14th century poet named Tulsidas wrote a simple, beautiful poem about Hanuman. It's called the *Hanuman Chaaleesa* for its forty stanzas —"chaalees" in Hindi means "forty." Hanuman's line in my made-up story, "Ghosts and demons come not near," is a translation of a line from this poem.

—Uma Krishnaswami

Photo by Nikhil Krishnaswamy

Uma Krishnaswami was born in India and now lives in northwest New Mexico. The author of several children's books, including *Chachaji's Cup* (2004 Paterson Prize winner) and *Monsoon* (a Parents' Choice recommended book), among others, Uma is also co-director of the Bisti Writing Project in Farmington, New Mexico, a site of the National Writing Project.

To Katherine, Lucy, Stephanie, and Vaunda.
—U.K.

Photo by Kaustubh Sanghani

Shiraaz Bhabha was born and raised in Mumbai, India, and now lives in San Francisco, California. A gifted artist and web designer, Shiraaz had her first major show of paintings in Berkeley, California, in September of 2004. Her paintings blend Eastern and Western themes, techniques, and motifs. This is her first book for children.

To Mom and Dad for their constant love & guidance; to Kaustubh for his unconditional love, support, & understanding; to adorable baby Zephan for bringing new meaning to my life; and to my darling nephew Zayne.
—S.B.

Library of Congress Cataloging-in-Publication Data

Krishnaswami, Uma, 1956-
  The closet ghosts / story by Uma Krishnaswami; illustrations by Shiraaz Bhabha.
    p. cm.
  Summary: With help from Hanuman, the Hindu monkey god, Anu finds a way to cope with going to a new school, living in a new home, and even dealing with the mischievous ghosts in her closet.
  ISBN 0-89239-208-8 (hardcover)
  [1. Moving, Household—Fiction. 2. Ghosts—Fiction. 3. Hanuman (Hindu deity)—Fiction. 4. Hinduism—Fiction. 5. East Indian Americans—Fiction.] I. Bhabha, Shiraaz, ill. II. Title.
  PZ7.K8978Cl 2005
  [E]—dc22
                                                2005007517

Story copyright © 2006 by Uma Krishnaswami
Illustrations copyright © 2006 by Shiraaz Bhabha
Editor: Dana Goldberg
Design & Production: Carl Angel
Production Assistance: Janine Macbeth
Special thanks to Ina Cumpiano, Rosalyn Sheff, and the entire staff of Children's Book Press.

Distributed to the book trade by Publishers Group West. Quantity discounts available through the publisher for educational and nonprofit use.

Children's Book Press is a nonprofit publisher of multicultural and bilingual picture books. For a free catalog, write to: Children's Book Press, 2211 Mission Street, San Francisco, CA, 94110. Visit us on the web at: **www.childrensbookpress.org** A Teacher's Guide for this book is available on our website.

Printed in Hong Kong through Marwin Productions
10 9 8 7 6 5 4 3 2 1